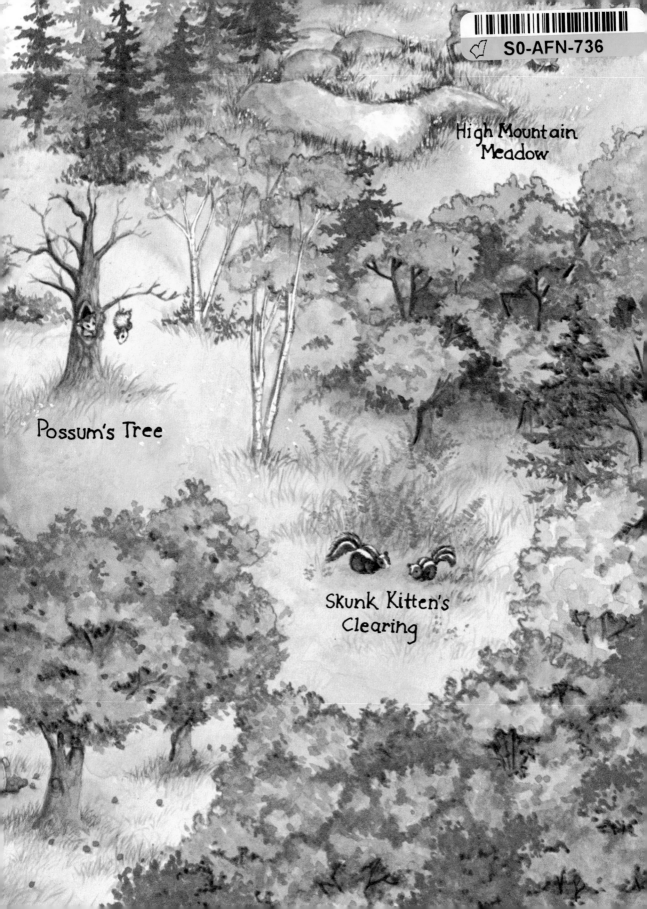

High Mountain
Meadow

Possum's Tree

Skunk Kitten's
Clearing

This book is a presentation of Weekly Reader Books.
Weekly Reader Books offers book clubs for children
from preschool through high school. For further
information write to: **Weekly Reader Books,**
4343 Equity Drive, Columbus, Ohio 43228.

Edited for Weekly Reader Books and published by
arrangement with Random House.

Library of Congress Cataloging in Publication Data: Ross, Katharine, 1950–   . The baby animals' party. SUMMARY: When a new baby
animal is born in the forest, all the other baby animals hurry to visit, each bringing a special gift. 1. Children's stories, American.
[1. Animals—Infancy—Fiction] I. McCue, Lisa, ill. II. Title. PZ7.R719693Bab 1986 [E] 84-43177
ISBN: 0-394-87355-6 (trade); 0-394-97355-0 (lib. bdg.)

Manufactured in the United States of America

Weekly Reader Children's Book Club presents

The Baby Animals' Party

by Katharine Ross
illustrated by Lisa McCue

Random House 🏠 New York

On a mild day,
at the high end of the forest,
in a thicket near a mountain meadow,
a baby was born.
Mockingbird flew over and saw the baby.
He swooped down into the valley
to tell everybody
about it.

When Raccoon Kitty heard,
he stopped washing the mountain perch
he had just pulled out of the stream.
He looked at his fresh fish and said,
"This will be my special present
for the new baby."
And he dunked the fish five times quickly—
dunk-dunk-dunk-dunk-dunk—
and slinked off across the forest
with the perch in his paw.

When Black Bear Cub heard the news,
she had her nose deep in the blackberry bush—
munch-munch-munching away
on juicy, fat blackberries warm from the sun.
She picked more berries
and a few more still, to eat along the way,
and lumbered off in search of the new baby.

When Cottontail Bunny heard,
he was crunching a yummy clump of dandelion weeds.
He sat up on his haunches
and twitched his nose.
So *that* was what he had smelled! New baby.
Cottontail Bunny bounded
about the clearing near his burrow,
picking dandelions and wild columbine
to make a surprise for the new baby.

Tiny Baby Chipmunk scampered to his cupboard
beneath the old, dead leaves.
He pulled out two hazelnuts,
five crispy pumpkin seeds,
and a pouchful of wild rice grains.
"I've been saving these especially
for a day like today.
Won't the new baby be pleased!"

Near the forest pond
Downy Duckling looked up and said,
"That new baby needs a nest!"
And she waddled among the rushes
gathering molted feathers
to fashion a cozy nest,
"like Mama Duck made me
and my eight duckling brothers and sisters."

In her globe of grass
in the sunken meadow
near the forest pond,
Tiniest Baby Field Mouse heard the news.
She knew just what to do.
She scampered to the old crabapple tree
and chose the ripest, reddest crabapple.
Then she rolled her ripe, red crabapple
all the way uphill to the baby.

Skunk Kitten went to his mother and said,
"If I promise not to spray,
can I go too?"
And Skunk Kitten's mother said,
"Of course you may go."
So he gathered up his beetles and his grasshoppers, too.
He gathered up his snakes and his smooth white turtle egg
and loped off after all the rest.

Shy Baby Possum,
high up in her tree,
looked down and saw,
passing one by one beneath her pointy nose—
Raccoon Kitty, Black Bear Cub,
Cottontail Bunny, Tiny Baby Chipmunk,
Downy Duckling, Tiniest Baby Field Mouse—
and even Skunk Kitten!
Baby Possum turned to her mother and said,
"I don't have anything to take the new baby.
I guess I can't go."
"Don't be silly," her mother replied.
"Hang upside down and make
that baby laugh.
Making a baby laugh is a
very important job."
Baby Possum dropped
to the ground
with her tail curled
up behind her
and hurried uphill after
the others.

And so, one after another,
the animals made their way
up the mountainside
to the high meadow
where Mockingbird said
they would find the new baby.
And sure enough,
in a thick cozy thicket
they found...

a newborn doe!
Mother Deer was standing proudly over her.
How they all stared!
Then, one by one, the baby animals
set their gifts down on the moss
before the newest baby animal of them all:

    Raccoon Kitty, his prize mountain perch;
    Black Bear Cub, her blackberries;
    Cottontail Bunny, a garland made of wild flowers;
    Tiny Baby Chipmunk, his hazelnuts, seeds, grains;
    Downy Duckling, the down for a feathered nest;
    Tiniest Baby Field Mouse, the ripe, red crabapple;
    Skunk Kitten, his bugs and snakes and turtle
    egg; and last but not least . . .

Shy Baby Possum crawled out on a branch
and hung upside down by her tail.
The doe stared and stared,
and started to giggle.
The giggle grew into a laugh,
and she laughed so hard that
she fell—*splat!*—on her face.
Her mother giggled and picked her up, and soon
everybody was laughing.
And that was just the beginning
of the most wonderful birthday party
that anyone can remember,
that mild afternoon,
at the high end of the forest,
in the mountain meadow,
the day the doe was born.